MW00888517

To Cynthia Platt and Mary Lee Donovan – J.M.
For Laura and Greta – J.D.

tiger tales
5 River Road, Suite 128, Wilton, CT 06897
Published in the United States 2013
Text copyright © 2013 Jamie Michalak
Illustrations copyright © 2013 Jon Davis
CIP data is available
ISBN-13: 978-1-58925-121-2
ISBN-10: 1-58925-121-0
Printed in China
TT/1400/0013/0313
All rights reserved
1 3 5 7 9 10 8 6 4 2

For more insight and activities,
visit us at www.tigertalesbooks.com

The Coziest Place

by Jamie Michalak

Illustrated by Jon Davis

tiger tales

At our backs, the wind is whipping.
Snow is falling, frost is nipping.

Toes are cold and noses rosy.
Time for us to go get cozy!

Cozy is our little home—
full of love, no need to roam.
Feeling toasty, safe, and snug,
wrapped up in a big bear hug.

Cozy is this time of day.
Snow on mittens melts away.

Cozy's dunking hot grilled cheese.
Cocoa topped with whipped cream, please!

Cozy are the comforts found
when all the family gathers round—
teddy bears and reading chairs. . .

soft and secret quilted lairs. . .

lazing by a roaring fire,

clothes just taken
from the dryer,
favorite pj's—
perfect fit!—

woolly socks
that Mama knit.

Cozy is the smell of baking.
What could Daddy Bear
be making?

Out come cookies!
Warm and sweet.

Just for us, a special treat.

Tummies full, we drift to bed,
dreams of sled rides in our heads.

Nestling under blanket heaps,
snuggling down to go to sleep.

Cozy is our little home—
full of love, no need to roam.

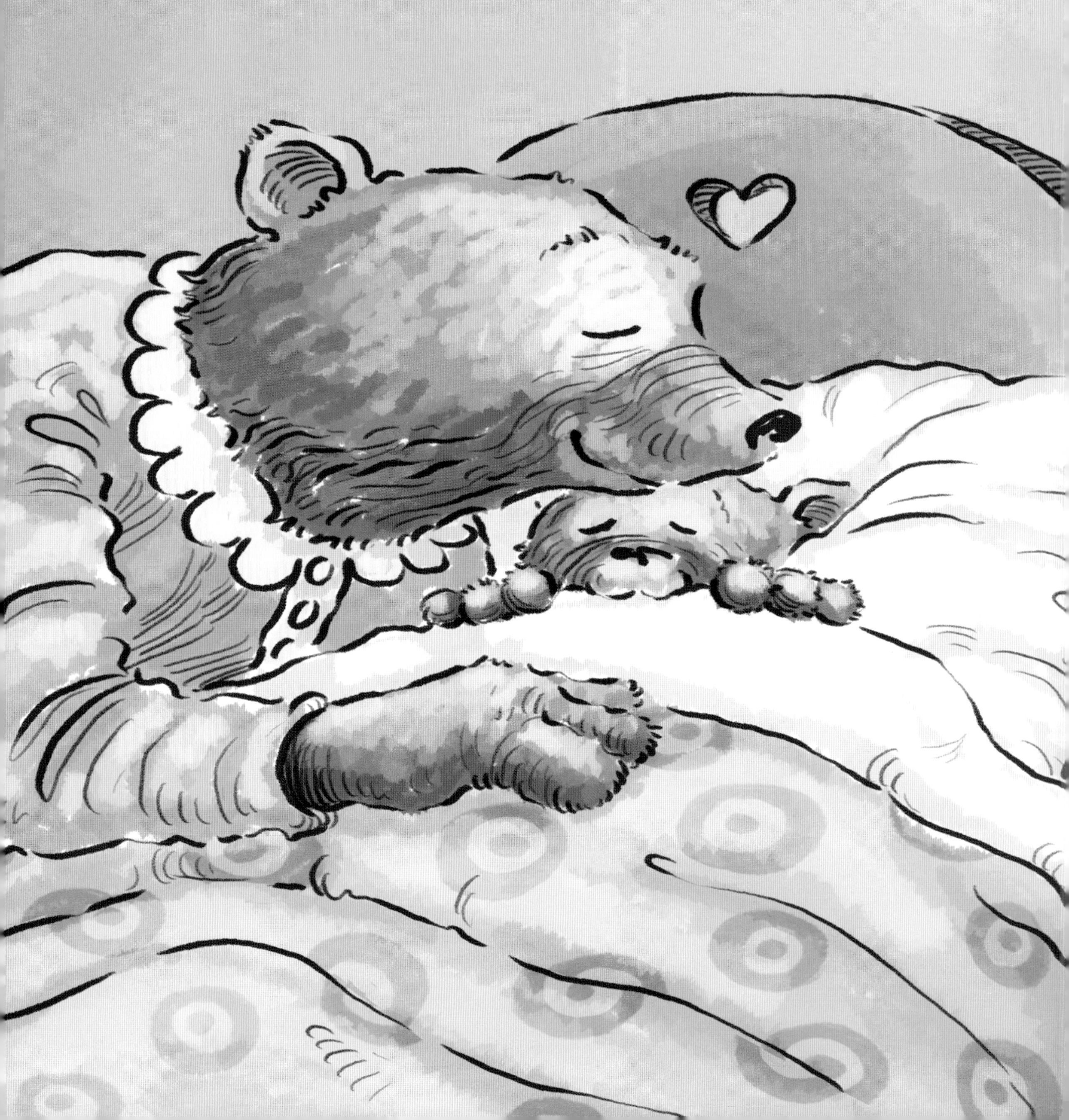

All is hushed. Off goes the light.
Time for bears to say "good night!"

S h h h h h !

Whoooooo!